MW00950320

## About the Author

María José Monge Lippa is a Costarican artist, journalist and Montessori guide. During her childhood, she, her sister Sofía, and childhood friend Michelle, played at each other's homes using their imaginations in the afternoons. They transformed ordinary spaces into adventurous locations. To this day they've never spent a boring day together.

# Just Imagine

**Written and Illustrated by Monge Lippa**

Just Imagine

Olympia Publishers
*London*

www.olympiapublishers.com
OLYMPIA PAPERBACK EDITION

Copyright © Monge Lippa 2020

The right of Monge Lippa to be identified as author of
this work has been asserted in accordance with sections 77 and 78 of the Copyright, Designs and Patents Act 1988.

All Rights Reserved

No reproduction, copy or transmission of this publication may be made without written permission.
No paragraph of this publication may be reproduced, copied or transmitted save with the written permission of the publisher, or in accordance with the provisions of the Copyright Act 1956 (as amended).

Any person who commits any unauthorised act in relation to
this publication may be liable to criminal prosecution and civil claims for damage.

A CIP catalogue record for this title is available from the British Library.

ISBN: 978-1-78830-807-6

First Published in 2020

Olympia Publishers
Tallis House
2 Tallis Street
London
EC4Y 0AB

Printed in Great Britain

# Dedication

To Sofía and Michelle, for always playing with me.

## Acknowledgements

Thank you to my family and my husband, Johnny, for supporting my ideas.

Did you know you could go anywhere you want?
Say a place and you can be there in no time!

You don't need a car or a plane,
a unicorn or a train,
all you really need is your brain!

Say "Alaska" for example,
you can make caves and
bears with no fuss, no hassle.

You can choose Paris,

or Iceland and see the Aurora Borealis!

There are so many things to see and do,
don't let boredom take them away from you!

When you want to visit a place,
you can be there, just transform a space.

Turn you living room into Peru!

Watch your couch become Kathmandu!

Go outside and make a jungle,
find the jaguars as you marvel.

See the wonders of the world.
There are no limits just say the word.

Say "Zimbabwe" or "Botswana".
But careful, a baboon may try to steal your banana!

Watch a stone become a bone and... BAM!
You're in Yellowstone!

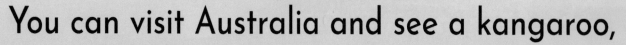

You can visit Australia and see a kangaroo,

or go to the place where a toilet is a 'loo'.

There is no place you cannot be,
your brain and where you are
is all you need, you see?

CPSIA information can be obtained
at www.ICGtesting.com
Printed in the USA
BVHW091916170820
586596BV00006B/334

9 781788 308076